To my little fishes: Sara, Miriam, Rivka, Deborah, Rajel, Mordejai, Arye, Yehuda, Yaacob, Chana, and Chaim, so they can always sing.

Sky Pony Press books may be purchased in bulk at special discounts for sales promotion, corporate gifts, fund-raising, or educational purposes. Special editions can also be created to specifications. For details, contact the Special Sales Department, Sky Pony Press, 307 West 36th Street, 11th Floor, New York, NY 10018 or info@skyhorsepublishing.com.

Sky Pony® is a registered trademark of Skyhorse Publishing, Inc.®, a Delaware corporation.

Visit our website at www.skyponypress.com.

10 9 8 7 6 5 4 3 2 1

Manufactured in China, July 2014
This product conforms to CPSIA 2008

Library of Congress Cataloging-in-Publication Data

Cohen, Santiago, author, illustrator.
The Yiddish fish / written and illustrated by Santiago Cohen.
pages cm
Summary: In Brooklyn a Yiddish-speaking fish escapes the fishmonger's knife.
ISBN 978-1-62914-633-1 (hardback)
[1. Fishes--Fiction. 2. Human-animal communication--Fiction. 3. Escapes--Fiction. 4. Jews--United States--Fiction. 5. Humorous stories.]
PZ7.C6643Yi 2014
[E]--dc23
2014021418

Cover design by Danielle Ceccolini
Cover illustration credit Santiago Cohen

Ebook ISBN 978-1-63220-234-5

THE YIDDISH FISH

Oy Vey

Words and art
by Santiago Cohen

Sky Pony Press
New York

He looked to see if
there were any speakers
hidden under the table.

But when the fish stood up and
stared straight into his eyes,
Rob really flew into a panic.

He ran to Mr. Lipshitz, his boss, to see if he knew what to do about the talking fish.

"Mr. Lipshitz!" Rob shouted. "Something fishy is happening!"

Mr. Lipshitz didn't like being interrupted, so he was not amused by Rob's story.

The fish wisely jumped back into the tank where it came from before the two crazy-eyed men chopped off its head.

Mr. Lipshitz tried to catch the fish, but it looked like all the others in the tank. They didn't know which one had the magic speaking powers.

But just in case it was really Aunt
Louise, Rob Costello and Mr.
Lipshitz decided that it would be
bad luck to kill any of the fish.

They drove all the way to New Jersey, to a lake Mr. Lipshitz used to visit as a child.

Rob Costello and Mr. Lipshitz
dumped the fish into the lake.

The two men were unsure if they actually heard or simply imagined a fish giggling just before it swam into the lake.

Hee, hee!
כי ,כי!

As Rob watched the school of fish in the pond, he thought he heard all of the fish laughing. He and Mr. Lipshitz sat down to enjoy the beautiful sunset, still not quite believing in the talking fish.

The lake and everything around it quieted down after nightfall.

But that night, the neighbors swore they could hear the singing of a klezmer tune coming from the lake.

And when they heard it, they didn't want the tune to end.

But after a while, all the fish became sleepy.

And it ended.

Author's Note

For a long time I have been interested in animal stories that appear in the media. I have collected newspaper clippings of all sorts, like the snake that traveled inside a VCR by mail from Minnesota to New Jersey; a flying bull that leaped over the fence of a bull-fight ring in Mexico; a turtle that jumped and fell from a tall building in Shanghai (surviving a ten-floor drop); the celebrity falcons of New York that lived in a fancy apartment on Fifth Avenue and got evicted; rats that saved lives by sniffing bombs for the army; pigeons that rode the New York City subway; baby elephants that survived falling in wells in Kenya; penguins that were kidnapped in Australia by teenagers; and a parrot that denounced a cheating girlfriend.

Out of all the stories I have collected over the years, however, I especially love the talking fish story from the *New York Times*. The article was written in a magical and funny way, with the reporter interviewing the main subjects who swore that the fish talked to them in Yiddish. The idea of a talking fish begging a fishmonger to save his life became the opening for my story.

Is it possible that fish can talk? Well, there is very strong evidence that supports that they definitely communicate among themselves.

There are different scientists around the world studying fish sounds and communication. Some scientists specialize in just the noises that fish make, like the Florida State University Coastal and Marine Laboratory of the Oceanographic Institute, which in the 1950s recorded the first sounds differentiating different species of fish. They made a collection of hundreds of sounds emitted by fish and compared them to each other.

Some scientists focus on the communication and meaning of fish sounds, like Dr. Ashlee Lillis, a marine ecologist at North Carolina State University. She is studying the sounds of fish and deep-sea organisms—where no light makes sound communication important to navigation and survival. Most of these scientists record the sounds in the ocean and document thumps, clicks, grunts, and calls, analyzing each of the sounds and gathering data to analyze important facts of oceanic life, including fish communication.

Increasingly, scientists are discovering unusual mechanisms by which fish make and hear secret whispers, grunts, and thumps to attract mates or to ward off enemies.

There are more than twenty-five thousand species of fish living today. Fish behaviorist Timothy Tricas at the University of Hawaii stated, "We know so far that at least one thousand fish species make sounds, with a huge diversity of means by which they generate and listen to sounds." "We also know butterfly fish swim very close together," Tricas said. "What we think might be happening is they are essentially whispering, and have to swim close together to listen." The fact that butterfly fish can effectively only whisper "may help explain the evolution of their pairing behavior, why the fish appear so social, and why almost all butterfly fish affiliate with one another so often."

Activity

1. Film and record sounds in a fish tank and try to analyze how the fish behave in certain situations.
2. Go online or to a library and research fish sounds and communication and see what you can learn.
3. Watch the reaction of various types of fish in a tank when different styles of music and noises are played. Film the reaction and compare each fish. Try different pleasant and strange noises.
4. Try different ways of communication with your friends by using different sounds or visual methods, just like a fish!

For more information you can read:

Hearing and Sound Communication in Fishes, edited by William N. Tavolga, Arthur Popper, and Richard R. Fay.

Fish Bioacoustics, by Jacqueline F. Webb, Arthur N. Popper, and Richard R. Fay.

Communication in Fishes, by Friedrich Ladich, Shaun P. Collin, Peter Moller, and B. G. Kapoor.

Sensory Processing in Aquatic Environments, by Shaun P. Collin and N. Justin Marshall.

Learning Their Language: Intuitive Communication with Animals and Nature, by Martha Williams.

Parent and Teacher web resources:

- Discovery of Sound in the Sea. This website will introduce students to the science and uses of sound in the sea: http://www.dosits.org

- The SeaDoc Society website works to protect the health of marine wildlife and their ecosystems through science and education: http://www.seadocsociety.org

- The Talking Fish website provides insight into the scientific, economic, and social aspects at work in New England's fisheries: http://www.talkingfish.org